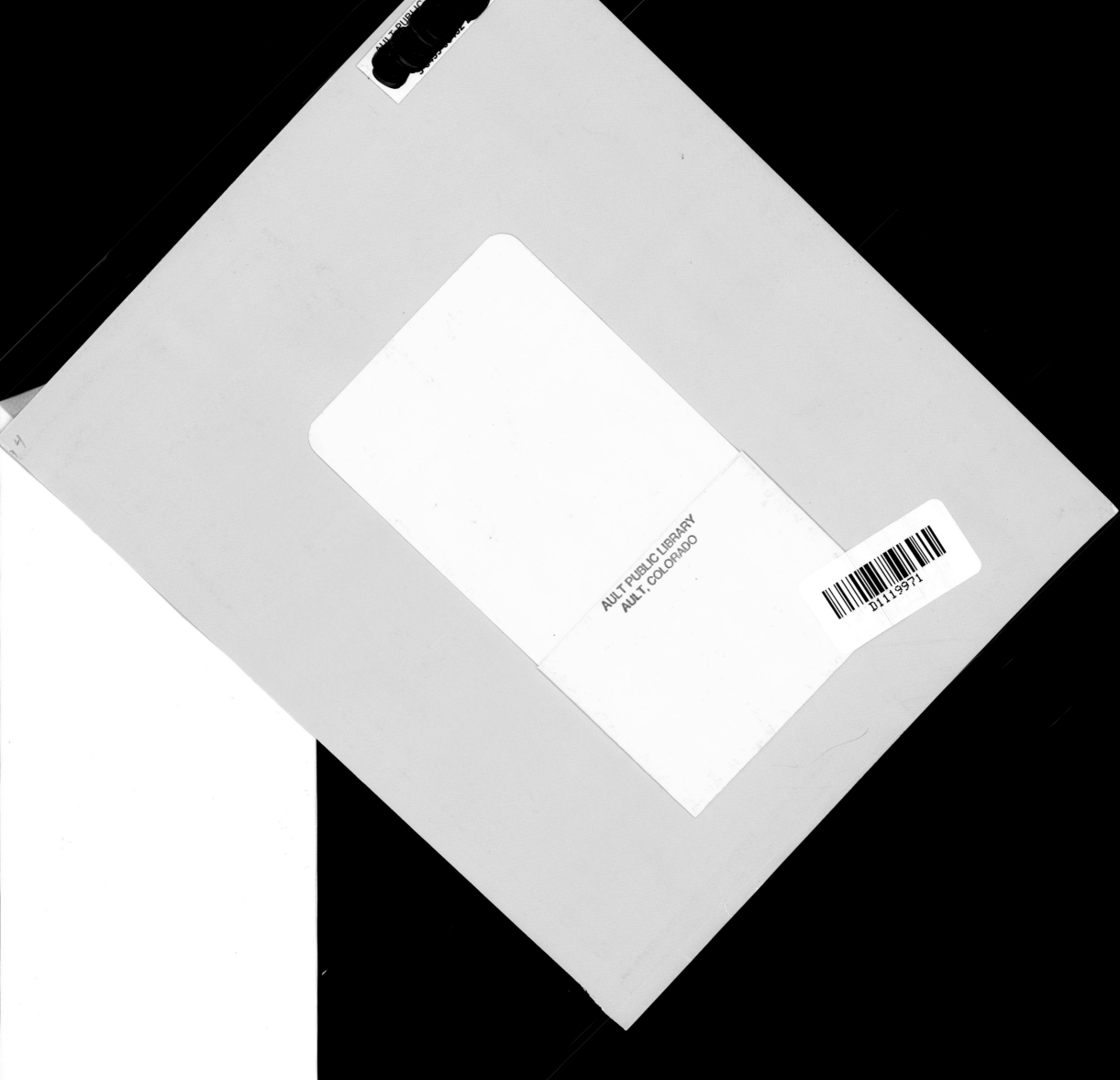

For Rita
and Brendan,
good friends

M.W.

For Paul,
Nick, and Emma,
my children

J.B.

Text copyright
© 1993 by Martin Waddell
Illustrations copyright
© 1993 by Jill Barton

First U.S. edition 1993
Published in
Great Britain in 1993 by
Walker Books Ltd., London.

Library of Congress
Cataloging-in-Publication Data is available.
ISBN 1-56402-211-0
Library of Congress
Catalog Card Number 92-54410

10 9 8 7 6 5 4 3 2 1

Printed in Hong Kong

The pictures in this book
were done in pencil and watercolor

Candlewick Press
2067 Massachusetts Avenue
Cambridge, Massachusetts 02140

$16.95 in Canada

The Happy Hedgehog Band
by Martin Waddell, illustrated by Jill Barton

"Waddell's . . . streamlined text is a pre-schooler's delight . . . and a captivating read-aloud. Young audiences will join eagerly in the fun and buzz, clap, hoot, click and drum along with Harry and his pals."—*Publishers Weekly*

"Barton's watercolor illustrations, rich in hues of green and brown, convey the exuberant joy of these woodland virtuosos. An ideal choice for preschool story hours." —*Booklist*

"The dependable Waddell's simple, expertly fashioned tale has just a touch of humor and is full of pleasing onomatopoeic words. Rendered in soft pencil and watercolor, Barton's creatures are truly engaging." —*Kirkus Reviews*

It's a crisp winter's day, and Little Mo decides to venture out onto the slippery ice. *BUMP!* Down she goes! *BUMP* again! Sliding isn't as easy as it looks. When the Big Ones come out to help, Little Mo finds she loves sliding and gliding and twisting and twirling with them. But when the fun becomes too rough for a small polar bear, Little Mo realizes that she doesn't really need Big Ones to show her how to have a good time.

Little ones will eagerly follow Little Mo's attempts to get her balance on her own as these warm and energetic illustrations capture the polar bears' lively winter fun.

E.

LITTLE
MO

Written by

Martin Waddell

Illustrated by

Jill Barton

CANDLEWICK PRESS
CAMBRIDGE, MASSACHUSETTS

Little Mo looked at the ice
and she liked it.

BUMP!

Little Mo got up   and tried sliding again.

BUMP!

A Big One came to help her.

More Big Ones came out onto the ice,

sliding and gliding around Little Mo.

They were her friends, all of them.

It was nice on the ice and she loved it.

The Big Ones whizzed and they whirled
and they twisted and twirled and
they raced and they jumped.

BUMP!

BUMP!

BUMP!

BUMP!

Little Mo started to cry and she turned away.
She didn't like the ice anymore.

"It was all *my* idea,"
Little Mo said to herself.

The Big Ones got tired and went home.

They forgot Little Mo.

Little Mo looked at the ice
and she liked it again.

She slid and. . .

she fell. *BUMP!*

She got up and then she
did it again without falling,   and again

and again   and again . . .

all by herself,
sliding around on the ice . . .

and Little Mo loved it.